THE WALKER BOOK OF
FUNNY STORIES

Also in this series

This collection first published 1995 as
A Walker Treasury: Funny Stories by Walker Books Ltd
87 Vauxhall Walk, London SE11 5HJ

This edition published 2000

4 6 8 10 9 7 5 3

Text © year of publication individual authors
Illustrations © year of publication individual authors
Cover illustration © 2000 Tony Ross

This book has been typeset in ITC Garamond

Printed in Great Britain by
Creative Print and Design (Wales), Ebbw Vale

British Library Cataloguing in Publication Data:
a catalogue record for this book is
available from the British Library

ISBN 0-7445-7739-X

www.walkerbooks.co.uk

The
Walker Book of
funny stories

WALKER BOOKS

AND SUBSIDIARIES

LONDON • BOSTON • SYDNEY

CONTENTS

MARY POGGS
AND THE
SUNSHINE

by VIVIAN FRENCH
illustrated by COLIN WEST

It was late summer, and everyone in the village of
Nornigig was sitting in the square talking about the
nearby village of Drumble Drone.

"Too clever by half, those old Drumblers," said
Tom Coddy gloomily.

"That's right," said Sal Slinpole. "Too clever by
half."

"Always thought as we were the cleverest," said
Sammy Chuffinhead. "But now see what they've
done. Put handles on their baskets, they have. Too
clever by half."

Tom, Sal and Sammy all sighed
heavily, and so did all the other
villagers.

Little Mary Poggs was sitting
beside Tom Coddy, rubbing
her chin.

"Why don't all of us Nornigigs build a fine tall building to show those old Drumblers how we're *much* the cleverest?" she said.

There was a long silence. Tom Coddy scratched his ear, and asked Sal Slinpole. Sal asked Sammy Chuffinhead, and the idea went all round the village, and everyone nodded and said, "Arrrr". But then came the big question: *What shall we build?* And even Mary Poggs couldn't think of an answer.

"We must ask Old Down," Mary said, and all the village agreed that that was the thing they must do.

Now, Old Down was a thinker. He was long in his thinking, and slow, but everyone in the village knew that if you wanted the answer to a question you went to Old Down. You took a present with you and you were very polite and always said please, and told him what the problem was. After a day or two, or even a week or two if it was a difficult question, you went back with another present, and Old Down would tell you the answer.

Mary Poggs was very excited about going to see Old Down. It had been decided that this was such an important question that all the village should go, and every one of them was to bring a present. Mary thought hard, and decided on a bowl of ripe red apples.

She was rather disappointed when she saw that everyone else had had the same idea, but she polished her apples until they shone, and decorated them with fresh green leaves.

All the villagers trailed slowly up the hill to Old Down's tower. Mary led the way, carefully carrying her bowl of shining apples.

Old Down was sitting outside his tower in the sunshine. Mary waited until the last small villager had puffed his way up to the top of the hill, and then presented her gift. Old Down smiled.

"Those is pretty apples," he said.

"If you please, we all of us want to build a fine tall building," Mary said, "so we can show the Drumblers how clever we Nornigigs are. But we don't know what to build."

Old Down nodded. Each villager in turn placed his or her gift in front of him, and he watched the pile of apples grow higher and higher.

"No eggs or little soft cheesies?" he asked.

Mary Poggs thought he sounded rather peevish for such a wise old man, but she curtsied politely.

"When shall we come for the answer?" she asked.

"I'll be taking as long as I need," said Old Down, "but if there's one or two of you as wants to come along tomorrow, I'll see how it is with me. 'Tis a hard question, mind."

Mary curtsied again. "I'll be back tomorrow, and thank you ever so."

All the villagers followed her down the hill to their homes. "I'll be off to see Old Down early," Mary said as she skipped along the path.

The next day Mary went up the hill with Tom Coddy for company. They took a basket of new laid eggs, and Old Down was cheerful.

"I'm thinking well," he said. "Things is coming along nicely."

"Shall we come back tomorrow then?" Mary asked.

Old Down gazed at the sky. "Maybe the day after," he said.

Mary took Sal Slinpole with her on the next visit. Sal was carrying a bowl filled with soft cheese. Old Down smiled. "I'm thinking better and better. It's never been so quick to come before."

Mary clapped her hands. "You know what we can build?"

Old Down stopped smiling and sighed. "All of a rush, you little ones. 'Tis a hard question, and you must be patient."

Mary curtsied low. "I'm ever so sorry. We'll not come bothering you for a while." She and Sal turned to go, but Old Down coughed.

"Maybe tomorrow … or the day after," he said. "Like I says, things is coming well."

"Thank you *ever* so," said Mary, and she and Sal skipped and hopped all the way down the hill to spread the good news.

Sammy Chuffinhead came looking for Mary a day or two later.

"Here's a fine chucky hen," he said. "Shall you take it to him up there to help him with his thinking?"

Mary thanked him. "That's a fine present," she said. "The finest yet." She tucked the hen under her arm and set off on her own up the hill.

Old Down was sitting outside his tower as usual.

"If you please," Mary said, curtsying, "Sammy's sent you a chucky hen."

He waved an arm at Mary and she put the hen down in front of him. It clucked, and began pottering about happily.

"The answer's nearly come." Old Down spoke in a slow deep voice.

Mary gave a little gasp.

Old Down closed his eyes, and Mary held her breath.

"Tell me the tallest building as you can put your mind to." Old Down sounded as if he was talking in his sleep.

Mary shut her eyes, and thought hard. "My gran told me once of a tall church with a tall tower that tickled the sky."

Old Down let out a heavy sigh.

"Exactly so," he said. "Go and tell all of them down below."

"Thank you *ever* so," said Mary, curtsying her best curtsy. "A tall church with a tall tower. I'll tell them – and they'll be as pleased as pleased could be. There's

none of us could've thought of that." And she waved to Old Down and went hurrying off with the news.

The village of Nornigig had never been so busy. Everyone was sawing or chopping or chipping or hammering or hauling baskets of stones and planks of wood to the centre of the marketplace where the church was to stand.

"Those old Drumblers won't ever have anything

as fine," Mary said proudly as the walls grew higher and higher. Tom Coddy was too puffed to answer, but he nodded as he staggered past carrying a roof beam.

Up and up went the church. The walls were of wood and stones, and the roof and the tall tower were of wood. On the day the weathercock was put on the top of the tower a holiday was called.

"We should all go and sing in the church," said Mary Poggs. "And then we should have a great feast. And we should ask all the Drumblers to come along and see."

Everyone nodded.

Tom Coddy scratched his leg. "I'll be off to fetch them old Drumblers," he said. "I'll be back at sundown."

The villagers all lined up, with Mary at the front. Then the door of the church was flung open, and in they all marched. The smallest villager pulled the door shut behind him.

"Oh," said Mary.

"Ah," said all the villagers.

"It do be terrible dark in here," said someone.

And it was indeed terribly dark. None of them could see their hands in front of their faces.

"I think," said Mary Poggs, "that we forgot the windows."

"We did think to put in a fine big door," said Sal Slinpole.

"Where is it?" asked Sammy.

"Here," said Mary, and they all trooped out again.

They sat on the grass outside the church and stared at the walls.

"'Tis all your fault, Mary Poggs," said Sal. "You and your ideas. What'll those Drumblers say?"

17

"We ain't got time to ask Old Down, neither," said Sammy. "Them Drumblers will be here by sundown or thereabouts – here to laugh, I shouldn't wonder."

Mary was staring at the sky. Suddenly she jumped to her feet.

"Quick! I know what to do! Bring all your baskets and bowls and buckets out here on the grass! We'll fill them full of sunshine, and then we'll tip it out in the church … and it'll be as bright as day!"

There was silence. All the villagers looked at Mary with their eyes and mouths wide open.

"Come on," said Mary.

Once again everyone began rushing to and fro. All the baskets and bowls and buckets were laid outside in the sunshine and left to fill while the preparations for the feast went merrily on. Mary stood watch, and as the sun moved across the sky she turned the baskets so that no shade fell over them.

"Are they filled up?" Sammy asked, coming to peer in his basket.

"I reckon," said Mary. "We'd better start shutting the lids down and covering them over."

Sal and Sammy and Mary began to close up the baskets, and cover over the buckets and bowls.

The other villagers came to watch, and Mary organized them into a line. "Carry them ever so carefully," she said. "No tripping or spilling or dropping."

Carefully, step by slow step, the sunshine was carried into the dark church.

"When I say *Now,*" said Mary, "we'll let the sunshine out."

Everybody stood beside their bowl or bucket or basket, holding their breath.

"One, two, three – *now!*" Mary shouted.

There was a mighty rustling and rattling and clanging.

"Oh," said Mary.

"Ah," said all the villagers.

It was still terribly dark.

Mary shut her eyes very tightly. There was a sudden flash in her mind – a great flash of light.

"Of course!" she cried. "The sunshine's gone because the sun's gone down. It'll be here in the morning, sure as eggs is eggs."

"Of course it will," said the villagers, slapping each other on the back with relief. They picked up the baskets, buckets and bowls, and carried them out of the church.

"Be sure and keep the door shut on that sunshine," said Mary. "Or there'll be none left tomorrow."

The smallest villager scuttled out quickly and slammed the door behind him.

"What about them Drumblers?" asked Sammy.

"Sun's gone down already," said Mary firmly. "And that door must be kept shut. They'll see our church and tower by moonlight … no need for them to go inside."

Tom Coddy came hurrying into the square. "Here we come… My, what a sight for sore eyes that fine tall church do be!"

A crowd of Drumblers was close behind him. There were loud cries of *"Oooooh!"* and *"Aaaaaah!"* as they saw the wonderful church.

"You Nornigigs do surely be the cleverest of folks round these here whichways," said their mayor, nodding his head over and over again.

The Nornigigs puffed up with pride, and beamed at each other. All, that is, except Mary Poggs.

Mary Poggs was hurrying up the hillside towards Old Down's tower. In one hand she carried a basket heaped high with good things from the feast, in the other a candle to light her way in the darkness.

"Old Down!" she called.

Old Down stretched, and yawned, and looked up from his excellent supper of apples, cheese and eggs.

"Old Down," Mary said, hurriedly curtsying low. "Old Down, will sunshine keep safe overnight?"

Old Down rubbed his nose thoughtfully. "Ah," he said, "'tis a difficult question."

Mary pushed the piled-up basket of goodies into his arms. "Please," she begged, "I need to know terribly badly."

"'Tis too dark for thinking," Old Down said, peering into the basket. "I only think bright in the day, just like the sunshine. Bright as that there candle I am, come the day. Could you shine that over here so's I can see what you be a-bringing?"

Mary Poggs took no notice. She was staring at the candle, and smiling. "Candles can be as bright as any sun," she said to herself.

She jumped up.

"Thank you ever so, Old Down," she called as she hurried off down to the celebrations.

Old Down shook his head. "Darned if I can remember what that little Mary wanted to know," he said.

Mary Poggs enjoyed the feasting, and the singing, and the dancing. She had slipped into the church with fifty fine candles all ready for the morning, and she made a note that the stones in the wall under Tom Coddy's roof beam were very loose.

Might be a pretty place for a window, she thought to herself. And Mary Poggs knew that one day, when she was ready, she would find herself a tower on a hillside and sit in front of it and think.

"Old Poggs, they'll call me," she said to herself with a smile. "Wise Old Poggs."

And she skipped off to join in the dancing.

LITTLE LUIS
AND THE
BAD BANDIT

by ANN JUNGMAN
illustrated by RUSSELL AYTO

Long ago in Mexico there lived a wicked bandit called Mexican Pete. Mexican Pete had the longest mustachios and the biggest sombrero in all of Mexico, and everyone was afraid of him.

Everywhere there were posters offering a big reward to the person who captured Mexican Pete. When the bandit saw the posters, he just laughed and took out two of his many guns, and fired into the air.

People saw the grim pictures of Mexican Pete looking

27

down on them from the walls, and shook with fear. Only one person was not afraid of Mexican Pete – and that was Little Luis.

Luis was the son of the local landowner, Don Francisco Emilio de Garcia y Lopez. Every day, when Little Luis passed the poster of the bandit on his way to church and again on his way back, he would look at the picture and say, "Oh, this Señor Pete has such sad eyes. He is not a happy man."

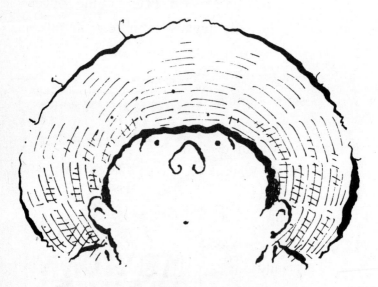

His father, Don Francisco, did not agree.

"That wicked bandit," he fumed over supper, "has stolen ten more of my cattle today!"

Little Luis wept into his soup.

"Why are you crying?" demanded his father. "Is it because I have had more cows stolen?"

"No, Papa," wept Little Luis, "it is because Señor Pete is so sad!"

"Sad!" shouted his father. "What do you mean, sad?"

"It is in his eyes, Papa. Señor Pete is not a happy man."

"What rubbish!" snapped his father.

Just then Isabella, Little Luis's sister, swept downstairs. She was so beautiful that she was known as the fair Isabellita.

"Papa!" she cried. "My jewels have gone! The ones that belonged to Mama!"

"It must be that bandit!" yelled her father, slamming his fist on the table. "This will have to stop. I will double the reward. Someone is bound to betray him."

Don Francisco was making so much noise that he didn't hear the sounds of people marching and shouting. Luis and Isabellita did and ran to the window.

"Papa," Little Luis said, "it is the villagers. They are all coming this way and they look very upset."

"It's that bandit, I'll be bound," declared his father. "Let them come in."

Soon the room was full of people all talking at once.

"Quiet," Don Francisco commanded. "One at a time. Now, Maria, what is it?"

"Oh, Don Francisco, all the watermelons I collected to sell in the market have been stolen. Oh, how will I feed my eight children?"

"Dry your tears, Maria," said Don Francisco. "Here is money for food."

"Now, Pancho. What has happened to you?"

"Don Francisco, both my goats have been stolen and there is no milk for anyone."

"More work of Mexican Pete, I warrant," said Don

Francisco. "Pancho, take one of my goats. And old Ramirez, what has this bandit taken of yours?"

"My medals from the war, Don Francisco, the one I fought in with your father. They were my pride and joy."

"Ramirez, don't cry. I will give you the medals that were my father's. Now, everyone listen: I, Don Francisco Emilio de Garcia y Lopez, promise you that soon this Mexican Pete will stop stealing from us."

The people cheered and went home feeling comforted.

Little Luis thought to himself, This Señor Pete, now he's stealing from the poor people. It will not do! My father can afford to lose some cattle and my sister can live without her jewels, but Maria's children cannot eat if her fruit is stolen.

The next day Little Luis stared at the poster of Mexican Pete for a bit longer than usual. All around, people were talking about the thefts and shaking their fists at the picture.

No one noticed that under a nearby tree a stranger lay asleep. He had a blanket over him and his sombrero covered his face.

For one moment he raised his hat and took a peep. It was only for a second, but when Little Luis saw his eyes he knew the stranger was none other than Mexican Pete.

Little Luis turned and said to Old Ramirez, who was very deaf, "Oh, Ramirez, I am very afraid of this wicked bandit. My father thinks he might kidnap me and has put away a lot of ransom money. That is why the reward for his capture is not higher! Oh, if I were this Señor Pete I would be tempted, very tempted!"

And Little Luis returned home, smiling to himself.

The next day, on his way to church, Little Luis suddenly felt an arm round him and then found himself lifted on to a horse.

"Tell your precious Don Francisco that I, Mexican Pete, have his son and I want the ransom!" shouted the bandit to the shocked villagers as he galloped off laughing.

Mexican Pete rode like lightning to his hideout. There he dumped Little Luis on the ground.

"You're nothing but a pipsqueak. All right, pipsqueak, go and collect some wood. We need a

fire. But don't try to escape if you know what is good for you!"

"Oh, no, Señor Pete," said Little Luis. "I am too afraid!"

And he put out his hand and patted the bandit's horse. Suddenly, without any warning, the horse reared up and …

dumped Mexican Pete into the river.

Little Luis helped him out. "Come on, Señor Pete, take my hand. Now you get those wet clothes off quickly and I will dry them on this rock."

So the bandit took off his soaking clothes and, growling, put on a new set. Then he climbed on to his horse.

"Right, pipsqueak," he said, "get a good fire going. I'm off to steal our supper."

Again Little Luis patted the horse and again the horse reared up and this time threw Mexican Pete into a pile of mud.

"Oh, Señor Pete!" cried Little Luis. "You are covered in mud. Take off those clothes and I will wash them in the river."

Little Luis trooped off with the dirty clothes, but

before he went he put a thorn under the saddle.

Mexican Pete, dressed in his last set of clothes, mounted his horse. The horse trotted a short distance and then flung Mexican Pete against a very spiky cactus.

"Oh, poor Señor Pete," cried Little Luis. "You are having no luck today. I think maybe you should forget about stealing our supper. No doubt there is something in the cave that I can cook."

Mexican Pete nodded. "That horse is going crazy," he muttered.

"It looks like it," agreed Little Luis. "What a good thing I am here to help, Señor Pete."

That night Little Luis and the bandit ate a simple meal of tortillas, or Mexican pancakes.

Mexican Pete was miserable. To cheer himself up he picked up his guitar and sang. Little Luis was amazed to hear such a glorious voice. It set him thinking: a voice like this should not just be heard by the cactus and the birds. Oh, how the people in the village would love to hear this singing.

"Oh, Señor Pete," he said, "how my sister, the fair Isabellita, would love to hear you sing."

"Isabellita is your sister? The girl with the black curls and the green eyes?"

"Yes, Señor Pete," said Little Luis, wiping away a tear. "She will be so worried about me. Señor Pete, would you deliver a short note to say that I am well?"

"I wouldn't want such a beautiful girl to worry," said the bandit. "But I might get caught."

"Oh, no, Señor Pete! If you shave off your mustachios and don't wear your very big sombrero, no one would recognize you."

"Shave off the best mustachios in Mexico? You must be crazy!"

"But my poor sister, Señor Pete. What of her?"

"For the peace of mind of a wonderful girl like that, the sacrifice of my mustachios is a small thing," declared the bandit. "But you must promise not to try to escape."

"Oh, Señor Pete," said Little Luis, "that is no problem. I like it here with you."

"You like it?"

"Oh, yes! At home I lead a very quiet life. This is exciting. If only I knew that poor Papa and Isabellita were not upset and worried, I would be very happy."

When night fell, the bandit leapt on to his horse.

Little Luis handed him the note.

"You look very good without the mustachios, Señor Pete. Now remember what I told you: if anyone asks your name, you are Señor Ernesto Gonzalez."

"If you say so," agreed the bandit.

And so Little Luis waved and smiled contentedly as the horse galloped off into the moonlight.

Mexican Pete, in a small sombrero and without mustachios, rode into the village. No one recognized him.

Mexican Pete stood under the poster with his picture on it. No one recognized him.

Mexican Pete had a drink in the local café. No one recognized him.

All around, people were talking about the kidnapping of Little Luis. Mexican Pete felt bad. "I am a very bad man," he said to himself.

Then Mexican Pete picked up his guitar and went to the house of Don Francisco Emilio de Garcia y Lopez. As he walked through the gardens, he heard the sound of weeping. He looked up and saw the fair Isabellita, in tears. Downstairs, Don Francisco Emilio de Garcia y Lopez sat in despair.

"I make everyone unhappy," said Mexican Pete to himself. "And I am unhappy, too. I must let Isabellita know that her little brother is safe."

Then Mexican Pete began to serenade the fair Isabellita:

In the mountains far away,
A bandit took a boy to stay—
  Olé olé olé olé.

But the boy is well and spry,
He tells his sister
    not to cry—
Olé olé olé olé.

The boy will be home soon,
Well before the next
    full moon—

Olé olé oléeee...
Olé olé oléeeeee!

Isabellita stopped crying and leaned over the balcony. "Señor, you have seen my brother?"

"Oh, yes, Señorita." Mexican Pete reached up and handed her the note.

"He is the prisoner of the bad bandit. But I, Ernesto Gonzalez, will rescue him."

"Oh, Señor Gonzalez! How happy you have made me!"

Mexican Pete bowed low. "Tomorrow I will return with your brother."

"Señor Gonzalez, when you and Luis come back, will you sing for me again?"

"Señorita, it will be an honour."

Mexican Pete mounted his horse and disappeared into the darkness.

When he got back to camp, Little Luis had steaming coffee all ready. They drank and Mexican Pete said, "I have been a bad man, Little Luis, a very bad man."

Little Luis nodded.

"But the beauty of your sister and the grief of the village people have moved me. Also, I am lonely. I do not like living alone in a cave. My horse keeps going crazy and throwing me into the river and so on. I will give up being a bandit and become a good man instead."

"Oh, Señor Pete, you make me very happy," cried Little Luis and he gave the bandit a big kiss. "We must pack up everything you stole and give it back."

"The people will never forgive me. I will have to spend the rest of my life in prison." Mexican Pete looked sad.

"Oh, no!" said Little Luis. "You are now Señor Ernesto Gonzalez and you have just rescued me from that wicked bandit!"

Mexican Pete was astonished. "You mean you would pretend that I am not Mexican Pete?"

"Yes, of course, Señor Gonzalez." Little Luis smiled. "Now let's go! Pronto!"

The next day Señor Ernesto Gonzalez and Little Luis rode into the village. When the people saw Little Luis they cheered. The cheers brought Isabellita and her father rushing into the square.

And that night there was a great feast. Everyone gathered round while Little Luis told his story about how Señor Ernesto Gonzalez rescued him from Mexican Pete's hideout.

Señor Ernesto sang for the crowd. Everyone loved it, but no one more than the fair Isabellita.

Señor Ernesto turned out to be a very good man. On Sundays he sang in the choir, and in the week he captured wild horses and sold them at a fair price. He taught the children how to ride and how to sing. After work he helped people in the fields and in their houses.

Sometimes he even did the washing-up.

"How can we persuade this Señor Ernesto Gonzalez to stay in our village?" the people asked.

Isabellita knew. "I think I can persuade him to stay," she said.

The next time Señor Ernesto Gonzalez sang under Isabellita's window, she threw him a flower – which told Señor Ernesto that he could ask for her hand in marriage. Don Francisco was very happy with the idea and later that summer Señor Ernesto Gonzalez and the fair Isabellita were married.

As the couple knelt before the priest, Little Luis gave a sigh. "Oh, I like this Señor Ernesto, who is to be my brother-in-law," he said. "He is a good man!"

KARI

by ROBERT LEESON
illustrated by AXEL SCHEFFLER

Kari was raking the hay in the big meadow on Haugen's farm one summer day, and thinking about the kind of things girls think of at hay-making time.

All of a sudden she had the feeling she was being watched. And so she was. For Haugen himself stood there, stout and whiskery, waistcoat creased over his broad middle, round hat over his white curls and long curved pipe in his gnarled fingers.

"Hey there, Kari," he said in a very agreeable manner. That put her on her guard right away.

"Good day, Farmer Haugen," she said and went on with her raking. She wished he'd go away, but he didn't. He stood there watching her, and smiling.

"Ha hm," said Haugen, clearing his throat. Kari stopped raking and looked up at him. It didn't seem polite to go on working when he clearly had something to say.

"What do you think, Kari?" he went on. "I've been thinking of getting married again."

So that was the way the wind blew, thought Kari. She had a little giggle to herself, because Haugen was a widower and as old as the hills. But she said demurely, "People do think about things like that."

"Ha hm," went on the farmer. "The point is, I thought about marrying you."

Oh ho, said Kari to herself, as if the old goat hasn't got enough to do without getting married again. But aloud she said, very politely, "Thank you very much, Farmer Haugen, but no thank you."

There was a deep silence. When Kari looked up again she saw his broad back going away up the meadow towards the farmhouse. When he was far away enough, she had a good laugh and went on raking the hay.

But if Kari imagined that was the end of the matter she was very much mistaken. Before the month was out, Farmer Haugen had asked her again, and again. Because he was a man who wasn't used to being told no. People usually did what he asked or told them.

And since Kari had to work for him now and then to earn money to help her family, maybe he felt she was obliged to him. But she kept on turning him down, very courteously but very firmly. Because if she had thought of getting married (and she kept that to herself) she wasn't going to marry him.

Still he didn't give up.

The next thing that happened was that Kari's father, whose smallholding lay next to Haugen's big farm, spoke to her one evening.

"Kari, dear. You're a very lucky girl. There's any amount of women in this valley who'd give their eyeteeth to marry Farmer Haugen."

"Well, let them do it, Dad," responded Kari, "and good luck to them."

"But he's the richest farmer for miles around. He's got a chest full of silver, and even got money down in the bank in town. He's a real catch."

"I don't care if he's up to his eyebrows in gold," said his daughter. "He's as old as the hills, he's as ugly as sin, and I don't want to marry him."

Now her father tried being angry with her.

"You're only a child, girl. You don't know what's good for you."

"I know what's bad for me," returned Kari, very firmly, "and I'm not marrying him."

And he said no more because he knew his daughter well enough not to waste his time.

Kari went on with her work, on Haugen's big farm and her father's small one. The days passed, and she heard no more about marriage.

But Haugen was only waiting his chance. He told his neighbour that it would be worth his while to persuade the girl one way or another.

"You know that piece of land which lies next to

your meadow? That's yours the day you get her to say yes."

So Kari's father was determined she should marry the rich neighbour and she was determined she wouldn't. In the end, after several attempts to make her see reason, he thought of a smart idea and he sent word to Haugen.

"Just you go ahead and arrange the wedding feast. Get the priest there and your guests. Then send word you want Kari at your place to do some work.

"When she comes, marry her, on the spot, before she has time to think. After all, she's very young. She doesn't really know her own mind. We know what's best for her."

Haugen was delighted with the scheme and set about fixing matters with the priest, inviting guests and all. He told his farm people to brew and bake and make ready for the biggest wedding celebration the valley had seen in a lifetime. And so they did.

At last the day came, a bright summer day. The guests arrived and the rich farmer had them all assembled in his best room, ready for the bride to arrive. The priest was there with his book, the kitchen tables were loaded with food and drink. Everything was as it should be.

Now Haugen called one of his boys and said, tapping his nose with his finger, "Now off you get to the neighbour, you know, Kari's father and – listen carefully – ask him for what he promised me."

Then he shook his huge fist and said, "Shift yourself. If you're not back in a jiffy, I'll—" He said no more, but the farm lad took one look at the fist and he was off out of the yard as if his pants were on fire.

Kari's father was waiting for him, and when the boy gave the message he nodded knowingly and said, "You nip down to the meadow and take her with you … you'll find her down there."

The lad was getting a bit muddled now, but did as he was told, though he hadn't the faintest notion what he was to take. So he was relieved when he got down to the little meadow and found Kari there.

"Kari," said he.

"Hey there," she answered, giving him a strange look. "What's all the rush about?"

"I've to fetch what your dad promised the master," he said, making sure he got the message right.

Oh ho, who's fooling who? thought Kari. But she told the boy, "Let's see. That must mean the old dun mare, eh?"

He shrugged and supposed it must be.

She grinned.

"Well, she's over the other
side of the pea patch, tied up.
You take her." And she added,
"Don't keep 'em waiting."

So the farm lad ran, untied the old dun mare,
sprang on her back and rode like a jockey across the
fields to Haugen's big farmhouse.

He found his master waiting impatiently outside
the big room full of chattering guests.

"Where is she?" the farmer demanded. The boy
took one look at the fist and decided to say as little
as possible.

"Down by the door," he answered.

"Right, now take her to my mother's old room
upstairs."

"Hey, how am I going to do that?" blurted the boy.

"Just do as I say," said his master. "And if you can't
handle her by yourself, get some of the fellers to help
you." He tapped his nose again. "We don't want her
doing herself a mischief."

The lad took one look at the farmer's face and
decided not to argue. Down he went to the yard and
got all the help he could gather. Some men pulled
from the front and some shoved from the back and

at last they got the mare up the stairs and into the room. There, on the old bed, was all the wedding finery spread out.

Shaking his head, the boy went back to the master.

"Well, it's done, but it was a struggle, I can tell you – the worst job I've had on this farm."

Haugen got his meaning. "All right, lad, your work won't be for nothing, don't worry. Now, get the girls from the kitchen and send them upstairs to help her get ready."

"You what?" the boy was quite bewildered.

"Don't argue," the farmer's face turned red with anger. "Do as I tell you. They've got to get her dressed and down here right away. And tell them not to forget the garlands and the crown."

So the boy didn't argue any more but went to the kitchen and said, "Now then, girls. You've to go up and dress the old dun mare in the wedding things."

They stared at him, so he explained on the spur of the moment.

"It must be some sort of joke he's playing on the guests."

Off went the girls and they dressed the old mare in all the finery, hanging on her everything they could find. When that was done, the boy went downstairs and told the master with a big wink, "She's ready."

"Very good," said the farmer. "Bring her down and I'll be at the door to welcome her. Hurry up."

The guests crowded into the doorway behind Haugen and waited. Then they heard a scuffling and a scraping, a tumbling and a tramping, a snorting and a clattering. Everyone looked at one another in amazement.

"Here she is," declared Haugen in triumph.

And into the room came the old dun mare, in silken shoes and white gown, wedding garland round her neck and crown stuck over her ears.

For a moment there was dead silence. Haugen's eyes were starting out of his head.

Then someone began to snigger, and some smiled, then others chuckled and others laughed till the whole place was in an uproar.

It all happened some time ago, but they do say that the farmer was so well pleased with his bride, he never popped the question to anyone ever again.

THE GREAT GOLDEN BELLY-BUTTON

by **MICHAEL ROSEN**
illustrated by **CAROLINE HOLDEN**

King Jabber sat listening to the concert. The Ding-a-ling Brothers were singing their song, "If I Was a Pudding, I'd Ask You to Be the Custard". Oh dear, it was the thirty-ninth time he'd heard it and he hadn't liked it the first time. Yawn, yawn, yawn.

Then Donk the jester came on and told jokes. They were all terrible – especially the long one about the pig that ate the king's underpants.

When Wizzo the wizard stood on the stage and said that he was going to take a rabbit and a donkey out of his hat, enough was enough. King Jabber stood up and said, "I can't stand any more of this rubbish. I want fun, I want laughter, I want … I want … egg on toast."

The entertainers hurried off the stage and Bradstock brought in the egg on toast. The toast was soggy. The egg was burnt. Or was it the other way round?

53

"I'm supposed to be the king around here," said Jabber. "I'm royal and regal and you're loyal and legal. I'm supposed to sit about and do nothing all day, you're supposed to be really glad you've got a king, even though I cost an enormous amount of money, and we're all supposed to be terribly, terribly happy. But what happens? I'm bored and the Ding-a-ling Brothers are still singing that stupid song about the pudding and the custard. What am I going to do, Bradstock?"

"First of all, sir, can I suggest that you wipe the egg off your chin? And then might I remind you, sir, of the Great Golden Belly-button you had made?"

"Yes, yes, yes, Bradstock. I do remember. What of it?"

"Well, sir," said Bradstock, "you don't seem to have found much use for it yet."

"Use? Use? You don't use a Great Golden Belly-button. It just is. I had it made because it's a good sight more fun than listening to Wizzo, Donk and the Ding-a-lings."

"I understand, sir," said Bradstock, "but I would like to suggest that you give it away, as a kind of prize. Whoever can make you laugh the most will win the Great Golden Belly-button."

"No, Bradstock, anyone can make me laugh. It's too easy. I've got a better idea. Whoever can tell the biggest lie will win the Great Golden Belly-button. How about that?"

"Excellent idea, sir!"

So the herald went out all around the country telling people, "Hear this! Hear this! Whoever can show themselves to be the biggest liar in all the land will receive the Great Golden Belly-button from the hands of King Jabber himself."

It wasn't long before the palace was packed with people telling lies.

There was the woman who said she had a horse that could say "sausages"; the man who said he had grass growing in his armpits; the woman who said she could swallow armchairs, and so on and so on.

Once again, King Jabber was getting bored.

"It's time we ended this stupid game of yours, Bradstock."

"Your stupid game, sir."

"Yours!"

"Yours!"

"Yours!"

Just then a voice piped up, "I'm here."

Bradstock and King Jabber looked round, and there stood a small girl with a bowl in her hand.

"Who are you?" asked the king.

"Oh, come on," said the girl, whose name was

Peggy. "You remember me, don't you? You owe me a hundred gold pieces. I've come to collect them in my bowl here. It did have  cornflakes in, but it's clean now."

"A hundred gold pieces? A hundred gold pieces?" said the king. "I've never seen you before in my life. I've never promised you any money and you're a liar to say I have."

"You promised. You did!"

"Did you hear that, Bradstock? Have you ever heard a liar like this little sprat? Get out of here, girl, before I set my dogs on you."

"Just hold it right there," said Peggy. "If you've never heard a liar like me before, then you must give me the Great Golden Belly-button."

"Ah. Er, well. Er, no…" said the king. "Of course I didn't mean you were really a liar. I, er…"

"Oh well, if I'm not a liar then give me my hundred pieces of gold," said Peggy.

There was silence. Bradstock waited to be given the order to set the dogs on her.

"Well, sock me sideways, the little sprat has done it!" said King Jabber. "Girl, the Great Golden Belly-button is yours. Give it to her, Bradstock."

Bradstock gave Peggy the Belly-button and she left the palace with it in her breakfast bowl.

"Stupid game you thought up there," said the king to Bradstock.

"Stupid game *you* thought up, sir," said Bradstock.

"No, *you* thought up."

"No, *you* thought up."

"*You* thought up."

"More egg on toast, sir?"

"I suppose so," said the king.

PAPPY MASHY

by KATHY HENDERSON
illustrated by CHRIS FISHER

Pappy Mashy always sat in the armchair.

It was the only comfortable chair. It was the only chair he could fit into. And he always read the newspaper.

The Mashy children – Josie, Rosie, Gemma, Lisa, Tracy, Lacey, Wayne, Elaine and little Arbuthnot Mashy – played mostly.

And Mammy Mashy did everything else.

She fed the cats, shook the mats, cooked the meals, hushed the squeals, kept bees, pruned the trees, taught the children their ABCs, fixed the roof, unblocked the drains, nursed the children's aches and pains, washed, ironed, knitted, sewed, sang songs, wrote letters, changed nappies, paid bills, went to the supermarket, mended punctures and read the bedtime story.

And when the older children were all safe in the

classrooms of Sloth Road School, the baby was with Lilly-next-door and Pappy Mashy had stumbled off to his office to turn over more papers at his desk all day, then she'd go out to her part-time job as a bus driver.

But she always made sure she was home in time to collect the children and say hello to Pappy as he sank into his armchair to read the evening papers. Of course.

"Leave him be," she'd say to the little ones as she cooked the supper with one hand and did the big ones' homework with the other. "Your father's had a hard day."

That was just the way things were.

Now, though he was fat, it wasn't that Pappy Mashy was a lazy man. It was just that he liked to read the newspaper. And over the years, as his family had grown larger and larger, so he had come to like reading the newspaper more and more.

By the time little Arbuthnot was born, Pappy Mashy didn't just read one newspaper like most people. He didn't just read two newspapers like some people. He read lots of newspapers. In fact he read every newspaper he could lay his hands on. There was: *The Smellygraph* and *The Chimes, The Despondent* and *The Daily Excess, The Flash* and *The Stars, The Morning Shout* and *The Evening Screech*.

And that was just to start with. You name it, he read it, from the first page to the last, every single word.

Pappy Mashy read so many newspapers that the paper-boy from the shop down the road had got a bad case of soggy legs from carrying them all and refused to deliver to number 23 any more.

So now, very early every morning, the Mashys' front door would open and out would come Josie, Rosie, Gemma, Lisa, Tracy, Lacey, Wayne, Elaine and little Arbuthnot, and they'd trot down the road to the newspaper shop and stagger back with a newspaper under each and every arm.

And though Pappy Mashy was too busy reading to play with them, too busy reading to talk to them, too busy reading even to notice them, it wasn't that he didn't love his children. It was only that he couldn't resist the comfortable chair and the pile of newspapers.

The Mashy children were a clever lot and as busy as bees. They helped their mum. They helped their dad, and they certainly stood out at school. Wayne and Elaine had nursery class helper badges for looking after the gerbils.

Tracy and Lacey loved dressing up.

Gemma specialized in weather forecasting.

Josie could do the crossword faster than her teacher, and knew more long words.

Lisa was into art and craft.

And Arbuthnot showed every sign of taking after his father.

And Rosie? Rosie with the red hair and the bright blue eyes was the cleverest of them all. She noticed things.

Now as the winter wore away and spring drew near Rosie did a lot of noticing.

She noticed that Mammy was getting thinner and thinner, while Pappy was getting fatter and fatter (so fat indeed that he could scarcely fit into the comfortable chair any more). And she noticed that Mammy was getting snappier and snappier, while Pappy was getting snoozier and snoozier.

So Rosie at least was not surprised when one morning Mammy Mashy just couldn't get up.

"I'm sorry," she said, lying there in her bed, and her face was pale, pale, pale. "I'b got a code id by dose ad an ache id by head ad I feel terrible."

Pappy Mashy was very worried. "I'm going to call the doctor," he said and thumped downstairs.

"Don't worry," said Josie. "We'll manage between us, won't we?"

"Yes," said Rosie, Gemma, Lisa, Tracy, Lacey, Wayne and Elaine in a chorus. Arbuthnot chuckled. "So stay in bed and have a good rest," said Rosie, leading them out.

A little while later Dr Porridge came to see Mammy Mashy. She spent a long time with her. On her way out she gave Pappy and the children their instructions: "She's to spend a week in bed," said Dr Porridge firmly, "a *whole* week. She's not to work,

not to be worried, she's not even to come downstairs. What she needs is lots of warm drinks and peace and quiet and sleep. Is that clear?"

Josie, Rosie, Gemma, Lisa, Tracy, Lacey, Wayne, Elaine and little Arbuthnot all nodded solemnly. Even Pappy Mashy nodded, but his eyes were sliding towards the pages of the *Isfahan Gazette*.

It was a desperate week.

Josie, Rosie, Gemma, Lisa, Tracy, Lacey, Wayne and Elaine worked like slaves, but no matter how hard they worked, still the dirty dishes piled up and the food supplies ran down and the drains got blocked and little Arbuthnot did unspeakable things when they weren't looking. And the tide of old newspapers rose and rose and swilled around the house, threatening to engulf them all.

Pappy Mashy did try. He got up in the morning. He went to bed at night. He carried trays of warm drinks up to Mammy. He even fetched his own newspapers.

But it took no more than a glimpse of his armchair for him to need a little read. And the little reads grew longer and longer until he was buried there almost as much as he had ever been.

"This will not *do!*" said Rosie to Josie on Thursday night, as they swept a mountain of old paper out into the back yard.

"I'll give you a hand when I've finished this," mumbled Pappy Mashy sheepishly from the depths of the comfortable chair.

Lacey was cross. "Humph!" she snorted. "He's just like the man in the story Mrs Bugwort told us at school, the man who was turned into stone."

"Except it's not stone he's been turned to," said Rosie, "it's newspaper!"

By Friday they had eaten scrambled eggs six nights in a row, so Josie made pancake batter instead.

There was a gloomy silence in the kitchen, and they could hear the sound of Pappy sinking deeper into his papers next door.

"If only we could get him out of his chair," said Rosie.

"We had Miss Gullet for craft yesterday," piped up Lisa from the doorway.

"Really, Lisa, is that all you can think about!" fretted Josie.

"Look out!" Elaine and Wayne staggered in with a pile of dirty washing. Wayne heaved it into the washing machine. Elaine lifted the box of soap out on to the worktop.

"And we did papiyaay mashaay," went on Lisa,

unconcerned, "and Miss Gullet says there's going to be a craft competition and that I should make something for it."

Just then, Arbuthnot emptied a bag of flour on to the floor with spectacular results. He chortled. The kitchen filled with a cloud of dust and Josie, Rosie and Elaine all threw themselves on the floor to clear up the mess.

Seeing that they were busy, Arbuthnot decided to improve the batter mix. He leant over to the box of soap powder, picked up a scoopful and emptied it into the mixing bowl.

The batter started to froth.

"Oh, no!" raged Josie, straightening up, her hair white with flour. "There goes supper and we haven't got any eggs left!"

It was Rosie to the rescue. "No use crying over spilt milk," she said, removing the revolting Arbuthnot to the living-room. Then she came back, picked up the mixing bowl and emptied it into the rubbish bin.

Lisa stared into the bin. Then she did something very odd. Instead of putting the lid back on, she reached her hand into the sticky mess of batter and newspaper, and stirred.

"Yuk!" shrieked Josie. "That's disgusting! What are you doing?" Elaine made sick noises.

Lisa lifted her hand out and let blobs of batter and paper drip.

"It's a bit like Miss Gullet's papiyaay mashaay," she sang to herself with a little smile.

Rosie was noticing.

"Now I come to think of it," she said, "I seem to remember we did papier mâché when we were in Miss Gullet's too…"

Josie looked at them both as if they were mad.

"…and you can make models and things with it, can't you?"

"I'm hungry," wailed Wayne.

"All it is, is newspaper and flour-and-water paste, like batter without the eggs," said Lisa.

"And it goes all hard… As hard as stone," said Rosie thoughtfully.

"That's it!" she said, picking up a handful of gloop out of the bin. "Bother housework. I know what we're going to do!"

And Rosie danced a war dance on the sticky kitchen floor.

So it was cold baked beans for supper, and Pappy didn't even notice. He was too busy reading the *Bogota Bulletin*.

"We'll clear up, Pappy," said Josie when they'd

finished. "You take this hot drink up to Mum and keep her company for the evening." And Pappy, his nose still in his paper, obeyed like a lamb.

Then the fun began.

Such a ripping and tearing, a giggling and a scrunching you never did hear. Every waste-paper basket was emptied, every paper pile was plundered and soon the whole ground floor of number 23 was filled with shreds and strips of torn newspaper.

Out in the kitchen Josie and Gemma beat buckets full of batter.

Arbuthnot played snowstorms in the hall, and Rosie and Lisa were hard at work dismantling the old rabbit run and twisting the chicken wire that covered it into a strangely familiar shape.

All night long they worked, pasting and patting, slopping and sticking, while Arbuthnot slept in a nest of cushions.

And when the first blackbird sang from the next-door TV aerial, there was not a single newspaper, not even the tiniest shred of newspaper to be seen anywhere.

Josie, Rosie, Gemma, Lisa, Tracy, Lacey, Wayne and Elaine picked up little Arbuthnot and tiptoed upstairs to bed as the first cars revved in the street outside.

When Pappy Mashy staggered downstairs next morning he thought he'd seen a ghost.

It wasn't just that the house was tidy. Nor even that there wasn't a single heap of newspapers to be seen.

It was THAT!

There in his armchair, the only comfortable armchair, in fact the only chair he could fit into nowadays, there was something … someone … sitting … and reading … *his* newspaper!

Little Arbuthnot bumped down the stairs and landed at his feet.

"Pappy," said Arbuthnot, stretching out his arms, and in his amazement Pappy Mashy actually bent down and picked him up! Arbuthnot gurgled happily and clapped his hands, and Pappy became aware of a whole circle of sleepy children standing round him.

For the first time in a long time, Pappy Mashy looked straight at his children. They looked back expectantly.

Then, feeling weak at the knees with so much effort, he turned towards his chair again, and groaned.

"Who *is* that?"

"IT'S PAPIER MÂCHÉ!" said the children in a chorus.

"Pappy Mashy?" whimpered Pappy. "But that's me!"

The children giggled.

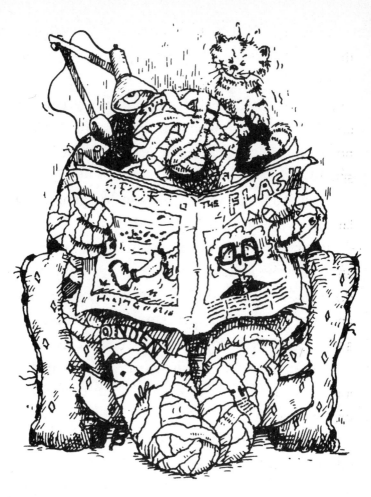

Pappy Mashy went over to the figure in the chair.

"May I have my newspaper?" he asked.

The figure didn't move.

Pappy took hold of the newspaper.

It wouldn't move either.

So Pappy pulled. The newspaper ripped.

"Well at least let me have my chair!"

Pappy took the figure firmly by the arms. He tugged, he shook, but all that happened was that the chair lifted off the ground. The figure was stuck fast.

And when he dropped it in despair, the whole lot landed on his foot.

Pappy hopped round the room in agony. The children were amazed. They couldn't ever remember him taking so much exercise in one morning.

But Tracy took no notice.

"Hey, Pappy," she said. "Come and look at this thing I've made, it's a superstrawbercoopercopter."

Pappy stopped hopping. "Huh?" he said.

And then he did another very unusual thing. Without a newspaper to read or a chair to sit in, Pappy *did* look.

In fact, he did more than look. He bent down and touched. Before long he was vrooming the superstrawbercoopercopter all over the newspaper-free floor. Wonder of wonders, Pappy was playing!

Pappy Mashy was so busy playing that he didn't hear the doorbell. He scarcely noticed Miss Gullet come in, and when he saw Josie and Rosie and Lisa help her carry *his* chair out to the car for the craft exhibition, he was having such a good time playing, that he just shrugged and waved.

"Phew!" he said as he mopped his face. "I haven't enjoyed myself so much for ages! Why don't you ask me to play with you more often?"

And Josie, Rosie, Gemma, Lisa, Tracy, Lacey, Wayne, Elaine and little Arbuthnot all laughed.

That afternoon Mammy Mashy came downstairs for the first time. She was pale and weak but her face seemed rested. The dark lines under her eyes had gone and she looked somehow rounder than before.

"Well, well," she said as she looked around, "you have done a good job!" Pappy smirked as if he'd done it all himself. Josie kicked him. "But where's the big chair gone?"

"Big chair?" asked Pappy, as if he'd never heard of it (and indeed he had almost forgotten it already). "It's er..."

"Being redecorated," said Lisa firmly. And that was the end of that.

But Rosie was noticing as usual.

"Are you sure you're all right, Mum?" she said. "You look a bit shaky."

"I do feel a bit weak," admitted Mammy. "I think, if you don't mind, I'll just have a little sit down."

And she sat down in the second most comfortable chair and opened a book.

IMPOSSIBLE PARENTS

by BRIAN PATTEN
illustrated by ARTHUR ROBINS

This is Ben Norm's bomber jacket.

 These are Ben's trousers.

These are Ben's trainers.

 These are his sister Mary's jeans.

These are her boots.

These are some of Ben and Mary's whatsits.

Put them all together and you can see how good they looked.

Still, Ben and Mary liked fitting in with the other kids in school. They liked wearing the same kind of stuff as their friends, so long as it was fashionable and not *everybody* wore it.

But ... have you ever seen such a stupid ponytail as this one?

It belongs to their dad and dangles from the back of his head. It's so embarrassing! And it's filthy! If you shook it you'd get enough dandruff to fill a tin of talcum powder!

And what about the daft earring in the corner of his right nostril! It's disgusting!

What happens when he wants to blow his nose? Maybe he can't blow it – ever! Maybe the nose ring gets rusty when he has a cold and his nose drips!

"Ponytails belong on ponies, not adults," snorted Ben.

"And rings belong in bulls' noses, not in grown-ups' nostrils," said Mary. "If it rusts he'll get some dreadful farmyard disease, then he'll have to be put down."

Sometimes – and this is really gross – sometimes when he dressed up, he wore a disgusting multi-coloured *shellsuit!*

But that wasn't the worst of it. Not only did their dad have a ring through his nose, a ponytail and a disgusting shellsuit, he also wore a puce-coloured bobble hat and a black string vest with holes in it.

"You've got to be really tatty to have holes in a string vest," moaned Ben. "Can you think of anyone who looks worse than Dad?"

"Yes," said Mary. "Unfortunately I can."

This is their mum. In one of her most ordinary outfits. It's a fishnet body stocking! If you think that's weird you should see her when she's dressed for work. You should see what she wears for her job as a belly dancer!

And it wasn't only the way their mum and dad looked.

Dad would pick his nose and flick bogies at flies. Mum would practise belly dancing in front of the window, or take her shoes off and paint her toenails, which doesn't sound so bad – until you've smelt her feet. Every time she took her shoes off, the cat fainted.

It was Mary's least favourite person, Alice Frimp, who started all the children boasting about their parents.

"My mum's responsible for keeping Princess Diana's clothes looking fresh. She's a royal fashion consultant," Alice Frimp said in the playground.

"Well, my dad's a test pilot," said Charlie Buggins.

"My mum's a high-powered businesswoman who used to be a brain surgeon," boasted Mavis Mayhem.

"Mine's an opera singer," said Pattie Rotti.

Mary nearly told the truth. She nearly said her mum was a belly dancer. "Mine's a b-be-bel-ballet dancer!" she blurted.

Mary thought Alice Frimp was a real grub.

"Yes," said Ben, "and Dad's a fireman."

One day, Miss Jones their teacher said, "Don't forget, it's Parents' Day next Friday. I'm looking forward to meeting all your nice parents for the first time."

"I couldn't stand Alice Frimp or any of her horrible gang seeing Mum and Dad. They'll poke fun at me for ever. They'll wobble their bellies at me!" wailed Mary as they walked home.

Ben felt the same. He wished he hadn't said their dad was a fireman. You don't see many string-vested firemen in puce-coloured bobble hats who have ponytails and wear rings in their noses.

What if Dad absent-mindedly flicked a bogey at Miss Jones? It was the kind of thing he might do. And then he'd pick something from between his teeth – *with the same finger!*

Ben and Mary were mortified. Miss Jones would be nice to their parents, and pretend not to notice their nasty habits. But what would she really think, deep down inside?

There must be something they could do to stop the Dreaded Parents coming along to Parents' Day.

"It's simple," said Ben. "We won't tell them."

"OK," agreed Mary. "We'll keep Parents' Day a secret."

But their mum and dad already knew.

Every single parent had received a nice letter from Miss Jones.

"I'm going to dig coming to Parents' Day," Dad said.

"So am I," said Mum. "I'll wear my leather jacket – the one with the slashes – and my fishnet body stocking. You'll be proud of us."

That night Ben and Mary held a powwow in their bedroom. The first thing they decided to do was to tackle the problem of Dad.

At midnight, when Mr and Mrs Norm were snoring loudly, Ben and Mary sneaked into their parents' bedroom.

Mary had a pair of very sharp scissors. A few quick hacks, and off came Dad's disgusting ponytail.

Ben had a pair of bolt cutters from the garage. A few expert snips and off came Dad's nose ring.

Then they took his multi-coloured shellsuit from the cupboard and put it in the dustbin.

That was enough for one night.

When they went down to breakfast next morning, Mr Norm was sitting in the kitchen. He was completely bald and Mrs Norm was busy tattooing his head. She was using a pin dipped in red and black inks. When she'd finished, a blotchy spider's web with a big fat red spider covered his whole head. "I started losing my hair last night," said Mr Norm, "so I decided to shave it all off and let Mum use my head as a canvas."

"I've always fancied a bit of home tattooing," said Mum.

Ben and Mary were well depressed, but Mr Norm loved the tattoo. He flicked a bogey at a passing fly and sighed with pleasure.

Ben moaned. Mary moaned. There were only a few days left before Parents' Day! They were frantic! Why did they have such impossible parents?

At school nobody seemed very enthusiastic about Parents' Day. In fact everybody looked a bit worried. Even Mary's arch-enemy, Alice Frimp, who had started them all boasting about their parents, seemed worried.

I don't think my mum will be coming to Parents' Day after all.

I hope...er, I mean I think mine will be away as well.

"I'm looking forward to meeting your dad," said Charlie Buggins. "A real fireman!"

Ben blushed and felt very hot. He wished he'd not told a fib. And Mary nearly burst into tears. Alice Frimp was a triple grub, getting them all boasting!

Mary thought of the horrible humiliation she would feel if it were discovered that her mum was a belly dancer instead of a ballet dancer.

And there was only one day to go!

That night Ben and Mary sneaked back into their parents' bedroom.

They found Mrs Norm's wild blue glitter-wig and hid it behind the wardrobe, along with her disgusting snakeskin belt and her alligator-skin tap shoes.

Next they rummaged about in the cupboard.

They found her fishnet body stocking, which they

stuffed into a bin-bag along with her pink feather boa and belly dancer outfit. They threw in Mr Norm's puce-coloured bobble hat and his tatty old black string vest. Then they took the whole lot downstairs and dumped it in the dustbin.

When they went down to breakfast next morning, there was a policeman standing in the kitchen talking to Mr and Mrs Norm, who were both wrapped in towels.

"A wild blue glitter-wig, and a fishnet body stocking, you say, madam? And a nose ring, you say, sir? Stolen?"

"Yes," said Mr Norm. "It seems there's been a burglar prowling about the last few nights. He's obviously got good taste."

"It means I'll have nothing to wear for Parents' Day today!" wailed Mrs Norm. "And I so wanted to make a good impression."

"Ah, Parents' Day. That might explain a few things," said the policeman thoughtfully.

He turned to Mary and Ben and asked, "Are you two quite sure you don't know anything about this?"

They blushed bright red. Sweat trickled down their sides.

"We often get mysterious goings-on just before Parents' Day," he said. "Well, if I see any suspicious-looking people wearing a glitter-wig, a nose ring and a belly dancer's outfit I'll let you know."

Then he put his notebook away and left.

Mary and Ben were quite pleased with themselves. Their parents had nothing to wear now except towels, and they couldn't very well go to Parents' Day wrapped in towels. Ben and Mary left for school that morning with light hearts.

Two streets away from their house they saw the policeman again. He was peering into a dustbin outside Mavis Mayhem's door.

I don't care about anything as long as Alice Frimp doesn't get a chance to see Mum in any of her disgusting outfits.

What's he up to?

At school everyone looked happy again. Compared with how miserable they'd felt after the announcement of Parents' Day, they positively glowed.

Everyone looked a bit too pleased with themselves. They'd all been up to something, Mary was sure – but what? Could they possibly have been trying to stop *their* parents coming to Parents' Day? Surely not. Surely nobody else had impossible parents. Or did they?

"Quiet, now!" said Miss Jones. "You all know it's Parents' Day, so I want you to be on your best behaviour."

She looked at her watch. "They're coming soon," she said. Miss Jones seemed to know exactly what the children were thinking. She seemed to know exactly what was going to happen.

"Half an hour before the parents arrive..." said Miss Jones.

The children looked out of the windows.

"Fifteen minutes…" smiled Miss Jones. "Ten, nine, eight, seven, six, five, four, three, two…"

The classroom door burst open and Alice Frimp's mum rushed in. Everyone could tell by the uniform she wore that she worked in the Dry Cleaner's around the corner from Kensington Palace. So much for her being the princess's fashion consultant! Alice Frimp had fibbed!

But then so had Pattie Rotti fibbed. Her mum wasn't an opera singer.

And Charlie Buggins' dad wasn't a test pilot. He drove the wet-fish lorry. You could tell by the smell.

The parents piled in, one after the other.

Everybody thought everyone else's parents were amazing and wonderful and that only their own were impossible.

Then, last of all, Ben and Mary's parents stormed in. They had got their clothes out of the dustbin. Mrs Norm wore her belly-dancing costume and everyone thought she was the most amazing mum ever.

Miss Jones was very impressed. She'd always had a secret desire to be a belly dancer, so Mrs Norm showed her how to do it. She stood up on a desk and did an amazing dance.

Then Miss Jones tried. She was a natural.

"I'm giving up teaching this afternoon and becoming a belly dancer instead," she shouted. "Let's all have a party!"

So they did!

It was the most wonderful Parents' Day there had ever been.

A NIGHT TO REMEMBER

by DYAN SHELDON
illustrated by ROBERT CROWTHER

It was Christmas Eve. The night was crisp and cold, and the stars shone like fairy lights in a dark and cloudless sky. Father Christmas whistled as he marched out to the stable.

A small, thin figure stumbled behind him. This was Father Christmas's grandson, Sam.

Sam was having trouble walking because his boots were too big.

At the entrance to the barn, Father Christmas stopped. "Ho-ho-ho!" he said, gazing up at the glittering sky. He looked back at the stumbling figure.

"You know, Sam, this is going to be a night to remember."

Sam was digging snow from his boots. "I'm going to remember it, all right," he grumbled. "I'm going to catch a cold."

Father Christmas frowned. Sam was a very modern boy. He was so modern that he wasn't really interested in filling stockings or in driving through the night in a sleigh pulled by eight reindeer. He was interested in television and videos. He was interested in loud music.

Stop dawdling! This is the greatest night of your life.

Sam fell over in the snow. "I'm too young for this, Grandad!" he said.

"Too young? Nonsense. I was your age when I first went out. I couldn't wait to see the sights." He pulled open the stable doors. "The pine trees of Toronto! The chimney-pots of London! The candles of Düsseldorf!"

Sam groaned. "But I don't care about the chimney-pots of London, Grandad. I'd rather see a film."

Father Christmas blew his nose. He had a bit of a cold himself. "What nonsense," he said.

Sam bumped into him with a cry of surprise. Sam was not only having trouble walking; he was having trouble seeing because his hat kept sliding over his eyes.

"Well, actually, Grandad…" he said hesitantly, "I'm not sure this is me."

"Not you?" Father Christmas flipped on the lights. "It's too much television," he said. "That's where you get these silly ideas."

Sam tripped into the barn. "It's just that I don't feel comfortable in this suit…"

He collided with a wall. "And I'm a little afraid of the deer…"

He stooped to retrieve the bells. "And I've never really liked riding in open sleighs…"

He shoved his hat back on his head.

"The trouble with you is you're lazy," said Father Christmas. He strode towards the back of the stable. "All you want to do is play video games all day."

Sam staggered after him. "It's not that, Grandad – " He bumped into a post. "I just don't think I'm cut out for this job. I've never really seen myself as a delivery boy…"

Father Christmas spun round. He looked closely at his grandson. It was true. He didn't look right. Perhaps Sam was going to be an even bigger disappointment than Father Christmas had feared.

"Delivery boy!" spluttered Father Christmas. "What do you mean, 'delivery boy'?" He pointed at the sleigh. "Father Christmas is not a delivery boy! He's jolly old St Nick and he brings happiness to millions of children all over the world!"

"I was hoping for a bit more fun," said Sam.

"And who said it isn't fun?" thundered Father Christmas.

"You did," said Sam. "You said you wanted a helper because you were bored with climbing over rooftops on your own. You said you were tired of lugging that heavy sack all by yourself."

Father Christmas straightened his hat. It was true, he *had* said that. He *was* a little bored with climbing over rooftops on his own. He *was* tired of lugging that heavy sack all by himself. Father Christmas frowned. He was sure that being St Nick used to be fun. He just couldn't seem to remember when.

"Never mind," said Father Christmas gruffly. "Fun isn't what matters. What matters is that there was nothing else I ever wanted to do."

"Well, I rather fancy being an astronaut," said Sam.

Father Christmas turned on his heel. "I'll get the deer," he said.

Together, Father Christmas and Sam harnessed the team.

"Not like that!" shouted Father Christmas. He wrenched the straps from his grandson's hands. "Can't you see you're making them nervous?"

Sam glanced over his shoulder. "They're making *me* nervous, Grandad," said Sam. "They look like hat racks and they smell like old socks. I don't know why we can't use a plane."

The reindeer's ears went up.

"Humph," said Father Christmas. Sam tried to help him load the sack on to the sleigh.

"Is that the way I showed you?" Father Christmas roared. He tugged the bag from Sam's grasp.

Sam collapsed with a groan. "No wonder you're always complaining about your back. That thing weighs a ton. Why can't we use a motorized cart?"

"Humph," said Father Christmas. "Get in."

Father Christmas and Sam took their places in the sleigh.

"Stop fidgeting!" ordered Father Christmas, giving his grandson a shove. "Why can't you sit still?"

"Because this seat's so hard and uncomfortable," said Sam. "Couldn't we at least get some cushions? This sleigh is like something out of the Stone Age."

The reindeer pawed the ground.

"Humph," said Father Christmas. "Let's go."

Together, Father Christmas and Sam began their journey round the world.

* * *

Father Christmas wouldn't let Sam drive. "You'll hit something," he said. "You'll go too fast. You'll crash."

Father Christmas wouldn't let Sam carry the sack. "You'll drop it," he said. "You'll fall off a roof."

Father Christmas wouldn't let Sam fill the stockings. "You'll break something," he said. "You'll mix things up."

Sam was chased up a tree in Toronto. He got stuck in a chimney in London. He was almost set on fire in Düsseldorf.

"You see!" fumed Father Christmas as they veered sharply towards the rooftops of Amsterdam. "You're completely useless."

Sam held on to his seat. "I'm not useless," he protested. "You're the one who won't let me do anything."

"Do anything?" repeated Father Christmas. They bounced over a row of houses. "What can *you* do besides turn on a television set?"

Sam held on tighter as the sleigh pitched and bucked. "I didn't *ask* to come," he managed to gasp. "I wish I'd stayed at home."

They skidded to a stop. Sam fell out of the sleigh.

"No!" raged Father Christmas. "I'm the one who wishes you'd stayed at home. This is the worst Christmas Eve I've ever known."

Sam pulled himself back into his seat. He pushed his hat out of his eyes and shook the snow out of his

hair. He looked around. "Uh, Grandad," said Sam. "Grandad, don't you think this roof is a little icy?"

"Icy?" shouted Father Christmas. "Of course it's icy! It's winter, isn't it?" He hurled himself from the driver's seat.

Sam looked for something to hold on to. "And steep," he added. "Icy and steep." He peered over the side. "And you've parked on a slope."

"Don't you tell me how to park!" Father Christmas yanked out the sack.

"But, Grandad," said Sam, "I really think…"

"I don't want to hear what you think!" snapped Father Christmas. He flung the enormous bag of toys over his shoulder.

"But if only you'd listen for a second…"

"Listen?" Father Christmas swung round. "I'll have you know that I've parked this sleigh more times than you've changed channels!"

"But, Grandad…"

"Let me tell you what *I* think, Sam Claus…" Father Christmas marched towards the chimney.

"Please be careful, Grandad!" called Sam.

"I think Comet would make a better jolly old St Nick than you. That's what I think!" Father Christmas roared.

And then he fell off the roof in a shower of gifts.

Sam brought the sleigh down to the ground. The reindeer watched as he helped his grandfather to his feet.

"Uh," grunted Father Christmas. "Ow." He limped to the sleigh, leaning on Sam. "Be careful," he groaned. "I've put my back out."

"I did try to warn you, Grandad," said Sam.

Father Christmas winced as he climbed into the sleigh.

Sam took off his hat and stuck it behind his grandfather's back. "If only we had some cushions…"

Father Christmas collapsed with a sigh. "Cushions are the least of our problems," he groaned. "Not only is this the worst Christmas Eve of my life, but it's going to be the worst Christmas Eve for a lot of children, too." He waved towards the presents scattered over the street. "I'll never get those presents delivered now."

The reindeer looked over their shoulders.

Sam looked at his grandfather.

Father Christmas looked at his sack, still caught in a tree. He shook his head sadly. "For the first time in hundreds of years, jolly old St Nick won't complete his rounds."

Sam cleared his throat. "Well ... I suppose *I* could always deliver the rest of the toys," he said softly.

"You?" asked Father Christmas. "You, Sam Claus, act as delivery boy? I thought you weren't cut out for this job."

"Maybe not," said Sam. "But I *am* here."

"Humph," said Father Christmas. "But you don't know what to do."

"I've watched you," said Sam. "I know what to do." He stepped out of the red suit. "And I'm getting rid of this, for a start."

"But you won't *look* like jolly old St Nick!" protested Father Christmas.

"No," said Sam. "I'll look like me."

The reindeer shuffled restlessly. They jingled their bells. They glared at Father Christmas.

Father Christmas glared back at the deer. "Oh, go ahead," he groaned. "I'm in too much pain to argue with any of you."

"Well, you were right about one thing," said Sam, tossing the suit into the back of the sleigh. "This is going to be a night to remember all right."

Contrary to what Father Christmas had feared, Sam didn't drop the sack, or break any presents, or mix up the toys. But he did sing as he filled the stockings. The reindeer tapped their feet and shook their bells.

Father Christmas lay back listening to the music in the air.

Suddenly Father Christmas saw himself as a boy.

He was lying on his bed, reading a book about sailing ships. He heard his father yelling at him for wasting his time.

Sam sprang from the chimney in a spray of snowdust. "You know, this isn't so bad after all," he called.

Father Christmas watched Sam spin before the stars. He saw himself as a boy, laughing and leaping down chimneys. He saw himself scattering presents and racing through the night. He heard his father complaining that he did everything wrong. He heard himself shouting that he wished he'd stayed at home.

"Wahoo!" Sam yelled as he climbed into the driver's seat and tugged at the reins. "You know," he laughed, "I think this is even better than being an astronaut."

Father Christmas leaned forward. "Did I ever tell you that there was a time when I thought I wanted to be a sailor?" he asked as they rose above the trees. It was something he'd forgotten himself.

Also contrary to what Father Christmas had feared, Sam didn't cause a crash. But he drove so fast that the wind whistled past them and the rooftops blurred.

The reindeer leapt over clouds and galloped through moonbeams. Sleigh-bells and laughter echoed through the night.

For the first time in months, Father Christmas wasn't tired. His bones didn't ache and his feet didn't hurt and he wasn't feeling the cold. He was having fun.

Sam looked down at the world shining below them. "There really are some great sights, aren't there," he said. He laughed as he guided the team round a tower.

"On, Dasher! On Dancer! On, Donner and Blitzen!" he cried.

"On, Comet! On Cupid! On Prancer and Vixen!" cried Father Christmas.

"Ho-ho-ho!" Sam roared.

"Ho-ho-ho!" roared his grandad.

The reindeer snorted, their bells rang out, and the sleigh sped across the moon.

"Merry Christmas, Sam!" laughed Father Christmas.

"Merry Christmas, Grandad!" laughed Sam.

"Merry Christmas to all!"

"And to all a good night!"

MILLIE MORGAN, PIRATE

by MARGARET RYAN
illustrated by CAROLINE CHURCH

"Heave to. Heave three. Drop the anchor. Drop everything!" yelled Millie Morgan, pirate captain (retired).

"Pardon?" said Griffon, her vulture and first mate. "If you want me to bring the *Seabird* to a standstill, why can't you just say STOP, Millie?"

But Millie Morgan, pirate captain (retired), wasn't listening. She was peering through her telescope at the nearest bit of dry land.

"Well, stab me vitals and loosen me corset," she said. "This telescope isn't working. I can hardly see a thing."

111

"That's because you've parked your bubble gum on the fat end again," said Griffon.

He peeled it off, and Millie said, "*Aar. Aar Aar. Aar Aar Aar,*" which roughly translated means: "Gosh, Griffon, that's much better. I can see now. Thanks very much."

"You're welcome," said Griffon.

"Lookee here, Griff," Millie went on. "Now that the rest of the crew have retired ashore, I think it's time we settled down too. Take a look at Little Drowsing by the Sea. Isn't it peaceful? My old bones tell me it's the perfect place for us."

Griffon looked.

"Perfect? It's perfectly awful. There are no cool cafés, no all-night chip shops, not even a take-away. And with Cookie gone ashore now too, I don't know if my stomach can stand any more of your cooking."

"Now don't get in a miff, Griff. Cast your eye over yonder to the harbour wall. What do you see there?"

112

Griffon cast his eye. "I see an old inn with very few walls and even less roof. I see a ruin."

"Isn't it wonderful?" said Millie. "Once we've fixed it up, it'll be just right for us to retire to."

"But Little Drowsing doesn't even have a hot dog stand," said Griffon. "Without Cookie I'll starve."

"I'll still cook for you," said Millie.

"I think I'd rather starve," said Griffon.

Millie bought the old inn from Mr Rookem, the estate agent in the high street. Griffon sighed as Millie handed over three large bags of gold doubloons in exchange for the keys. Not that they needed keys. They could walk in through the holes

in the walls or fly in through the holes in the roof.

But Millie was happy. She skipped about when she saw the inside of the inn.

"This be grand, Griffy," she said.

Griffon shook his bald head. "This be very far from grand, Millie. This be a right old mess."

"Keep your wig on, Griffy old mate. We'll soon have it all shipshape. Everything we need to fix the inn is on board the *Seabird*. Fly me over there and we'll start work right away."

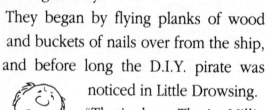

They began by flying planks of wood and buckets of nails over from the ship, and before long the D.I.Y. pirate was noticed in Little Drowsing.

"That's her. That's Millie Morgan, the fierce pirate," spluttered nosy Mrs Whinge, the postmistress, to nosy Mr Carp, the bank manager.

"I've just found out from Mr Rookem that she's bought The Old Inn. She's going to retire there. We must put a stop to that right away. We don't want *her* sort living in Little Drowsing."

"Quite right," said Mr Carp. "But let's move her on *after* she's rebuilt The Old Inn. She and that big bird are doing a good job. The old place looks better already."

And it did. Millie built up the walls while Griffon patched up the roof, and soon the inn was wind- and watertight. Then Millie put up a fence and a little white gate.

"It's looking good, Griffy old mate. Just the skull and crossbone curtains to hang up now. I'll do that while you fly over to the *Seabird* and bring back the brass cannon and the special ammunition."

"Expecting trouble, Millie?" asked Griffon.

"Well," said Millie. "I've noticed some lace curtains a-twitching and some beady eyes a-peering, and my old pirate bones tell me there's something afoot."

"You and your bones," muttered Griffon, but he went to collect the cannon and the special ammunition. Millie's bones were seldom wrong.

That evening, Millie and Griffon were sitting by a roaring fire toasting their toes and cracking their jaws on the disgusting beef stew Millie had made. She really was the worst cook in the world. Who else would make fish finger and treacle sandwiches or bake spaghetti and spinach cakes?

Griffon bravely swallowed a beakful of stew and felt it thud into his stomach.

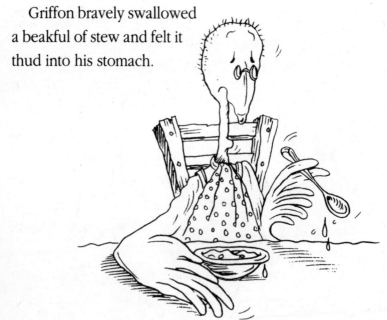

"Where have your spare seaboots gone, Millie?" he asked. "Are they in this stew?"

"Don't be daft, Griffy," said Millie. But she did wonder. She'd had to take the ship's axe to the meat to cut it up.

"If only Cookie were here," she sighed. "If only he hadn't retired to cook in that fancy restaurant. If only he were here to make us his steaming beef hotpot with fluffy, floury dumplings."

"And crunchy roast potatoes," said Griffon.

"And ice-cream gateau," said Millie.

"On a separate plate," said Griffon.

"Mmmmmmmmm," they both said. "Delicious."

Suddenly there was a sharp rap on the front door.

"Who can that be?" wondered Griffon.

Millie stood up and her bones creaked. "My old bones tell me that be trouble."

"Stop listening to your old bones and open the door."

Millie did. Mrs Whinge and Mr Carp stood on the doorstep.

"We've brought a petition signed by a great many people in Little Drowsing," said Mrs Whinge. "They

don't want the likes of you living here. They want you to leave."

"Leave?" Millie cried. "But I've only just got here. I've retired here. Scraped all the barnacles off me bottom and hung up me seaboots."

Mr Carp looked at Millie's bare toes.

"So I see," he said. "But you're not welcome. We don't want your sort here. So pack up your belongings and we'll be here first thing in the morning to see that you leave."

And Mrs Whinge and Mr Carp smiled nastily and left.

Millie showed the petition to Griffon. "Shivering shellfish," she said. "What a lot of people want us to go."

Griffon read the petition carefully all the way through, and he gave a hearty laugh. "Don't be a silly, Millie. That horrible pair have made this up between them. Just read the names."

Millie read the names:

Mrs Whinge	Mr Carp
Mr Whinge	Mrs Carp
Miss Whinge	Etta Carp
Master Whinge	Netta Carp
Rover Whinge	Tweetie Pie Carp
Tiddles Whinge	Goldie Carp

"Right, Griffy," said Millie. "Look out the special ammunition for the cannon. When that pair come round in the morning we'll be ready for them. Nobody messes with Millie Morgan and gets away with it."

Morning came early as usual, but Millie was up waiting for it, and Mrs Whinge and Mr Carp.

"Well," they said, marching up the path, "are you ready to leave?"

"Certainly not," said Millie. "But I think you might be. You can't fool Millie Morgan with your dirty tricks. Load the cannon, Griffy, and shiver their timbers! Wizzard their gizzards! Avast with the blast!"

Griffon sighed. "How about FIRE, Millie," he said.

"FIRE, MILLIE!" yelled Millie.

Griffon fired and millions of mouldy fish finger and treacle sandwiches, and stringy spaghetti and spinach cakes rained down on Mrs Whinge and Mr Carp.

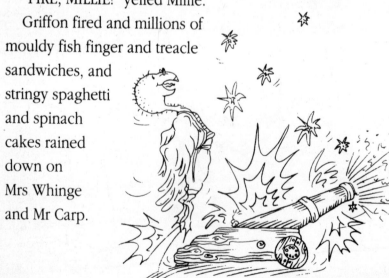

Zap. Splud. Sploink.

"Wowwwwwwl!" yelled Mr Carp.

Clunk. Boof. Doink.

"Owwwww!" yelled Mrs Whinge.

"And there's plenty more where those came from if you two ever come visiting again!" yelled Millie as they ran off down the path.

They were just going back indoors when a face peered over the fence. It had treacle and fish fingers stuck to its nose, and bits of spaghetti and spinach hanging from its pirate's hat.

"Cookie!" yelled Millie. "You're back." And she ran and kissed him.

SSSSLLLOOOOOOOOOOOOOOORRRPPP.

"Didn't like that fancy restaurant," said Cookie when he'd recovered. "Do you know, they wouldn't let me wear my pirate's hat in the kitchen? So I left and set off to find you. Luckily I knew which way you were headed.

I came round the corner just as the cannon fired the special ammunition. Then I knew I was home. Can I come and cook for you?"

"Of course," said Millie. "We could set up a fancy restaurant here, and call it The Jolly Lodger. That way you could wear your pirate's hat wherever you liked."

So that's what they did, and soon the restaurant became famous for miles around. To get in you had to come dressed as a pirate. The people of Little Drowsing thought this was great fun.

But one night two really fierce-looking pirates turned up. They wore black eye patches and big black beards. They thought nobody would recognize them under all that, but Millie would have known Mrs Whinge and Mr Carp anywhere.

"Ah, here be two really fierce pirates. We don't usually let your sort in, but if you promise to behave…"

Mrs Whinge and Mr Carp coughed and shuffled and they promised they would.

Millie held in a giggle as she served them large

pirate-sized helpings of steaming beef hotpot. After that, Mrs Whinge and Mr Carp came to the restaurant every Friday night. No one could resist Cookie's wonderful food.

Millie was delighted at how well things had turned out. "I knew this was the perfect place for us, Griffy," she said. "My old bones told me so."

But Griffon didn't reply. It's rude to speak with your mouth full.

THE BAKED BEAN KIDS

by ANN PILLING
illustrated by DEREK MATTHEWS

JOSS

The Baked Bean Kids were called Joss and Pin. Joss had a round face and stubby plaits. Her real name was Jocelyn but she didn't like it. It reminded her of glycerine, that sticky stuff which her mum sometimes poured into bubbling saucepans. Mum wrote cookery books and she was planning to be famous.

Joss didn't always like Pin. He was only little, but he was a big nuisance. He kept breaking her things. One day she stuck a notice on her bedroom door:

Pin hated secrets, and Joss was always having them. "My name's Edward," he grizzled.

"No, it's not, it's Pin," she said, and she wouldn't explain, except to her Very Secret Diary, which she wrote every night before she went to bed.

The worst thing about Pin was that he copied. When Joss got her new bike for her birthday he wanted one too.

When she got a kitten he wailed, "Give me one." When the dentist put a brace on her teeth he even wanted one of those as well!

Then she started collecting things – mugs and glass animals and rubbers in funny shapes.

Pin copied, but he collected silly things – the labels off tins, empty cornflakes boxes and unbent paperclips.

Joss was so fed up with Pin copying that she made an important decision. "I'm not telling anybody my plans from now on," she said to herself, and she wrote it in big letters in her Very Secret Diary.

But it was no use. Pin had this knack of finding out what she was up to and he found out about the baked beans. That's how the Shufflebottoms turned into the biggest bean-eaters this century.

squeak

It started the day that Mum had a big shout. When she got cross her voice went all squeaky. It made Joss want to laugh.

"It's no good," she yelled. "The bath's full of old cornflakes packets, and the goldfish bowl's full of paperclips. In fact this whole house is bursting at the seams with useless rubbish." (Squeak.) "If you've got to collect things can't it be something little? And why don't you collect proper things?" (Squeak, squeak.)

"You mean things I can keep for ever?" said Joss.

"Yes, for ever and ever." (Squeak.) "Now tidy up!"

Joss crept away and had a big think.

She started to tidy up Pin's bedroom. He was out, bouncing on Next Door's water bed. Tin labels: how boring, she thought, putting them in a neat pile.

128

Mum had said they should collect something little "that would last for ever and ever". But what did she mean? Buttons? Corks? Dried peas? Suddenly she stopped tidying. One of Pin's labels had caught her eye.

Joss started to read very carefully. She liked mints and Mum didn't let her eat sweets any more, because of her brace...

But it was nothing to do with mints. What you got for your fifty labels was a brand new set of coins, a penny, a five pence and a ten pence, everything, right up to a shiny gold pound. And none of them had ever been used.

Factory Fresh from the Famous London Mint, it said. You got a special book too, all about coin collecting.

Something little, that you could keep for ever and ever... This was the answer! They were doing a coin project at school and they were all supposed to bring "something interesting" to show the teacher. Joss folded up the beans label and put it into her pocket. One good thing about Mum's new cookery craze was that she was always going shopping. There'd be lots of tins of beans in the food cupboard already. She could just tear off the labels.

But there was a bad thing too; in fact there were two bad things. First, if Pin found out he'd copy. Second, Joss didn't really like baked beans.

Mum didn't have any tins of beans. And when Joss

asked her to buy fifty tins of Bigga's Best she said "No", just like that.

"Can I get mints too?" said Big Ears Pin, who'd sidled in from Next Door and heard every single word.

"Of course you can, poppet," Mum murmured, dreamily stirring something in a pan. Joss felt like killing her. This meant one hundred tins of beans.

It was OK at first. She could manage beans on toast, baked potatoes with beans, beans and chips.

131

The labels began to mount up. Not fast enough though. When a new supply of beans arrived Joss tore a few labels off the tins. Mum went mad.

"That's cheating," she said. (Squeak.) As a result, for that day Joss got *peas* for tea.

"Serve you right," said Mrs Shufflebottom. "You can buy the next lot of beans yourself."

Joss did. Next day she went straight down to Mr Banerjee's corner shop and bought three tins of Bigga's Best. The familiar red and yellow label was starting to make her feel a bit peculiar now, though. Every time she saw it her tummy seemed to puff up, like a balloon.

Mr Banerjee put the tins in a bag with a satisfied smile. He was fat – bigger than Mr Bigga, who did adverts on TV. "What's happening at your house?" he said. "Your mother's already bought six tins of beans this week. Is it for her cookery book?"

"Yes," Joss said. It wasn't, but Mr Banerjee had just given her a very good idea.

"Why don't you write a bean cookery book?" Joss said to Mum when she got home. Mum looked at her thoughtfully. Then she rooted among her recipe books and pulled out *Marvellous Meals With Mince*.

"You mean this kind of thing?"

"Why not?"

"All right. What shall we call it?"

"*Beans Give Me Burps*," suggested Pin.

He wouldn't eat them any more, but he still wanted his Special Mint Collection. *Typical.*

"No, darling, I don't think so," said his mother.

Joss studied the mince book. "How about *Brilliant Binges With Beans*?" she said.

"Mmm… Not sure… I know, let's call it *Bean Feast*. Short and sweet." And Mum started scribbling, straight away.

After that it was beans with everything: bean soup, bean stew, even bean sandwiches. These were really awful. Joss tried to get rid of them at school, but nobody seemed to want any. So she stuffed them behind the radiator.

That afternoon, in Projects, there was a funny bean smell wafting through the classroom. People started coughing and covering their noses with hankies. Hot fluff and beans was a disgusting combination.

* * *

Pin still refused to eat his beans up and Joss told him she wouldn't give him any labels unless he helped. So he sprinkled some in Fred's goldfish bowl.

The water instantly turned the colour of tomato soup. Then something peculiar happened. The goldfish normally did a sedate breast stroke, but after the beans he went mad and whizzed round and round. "He's doing the butterfly," said Pin.

Dad got worried. "He's only a little thing," he said, and he fished out all the beans with a spoon.

Every day Pin counted the labels to see if they'd

got enough. He grew impatient. Next news was that he'd fed some baked beans to the cats.

Albert, the ginger one, was small and timid; Victoria, the tabby, was a great big bully. She pushed him out of the way and gobbled the lot.

Very soon, though, she was sitting on top of the shed giving great howls, all swelled up like something out of a monster book.

She didn't come down from the roof for two days and when Mum got the tin opener out she took one look at the red and yellow label and tore off, back to the shed. "She can read," Pin said proudly.

One morning Mum went off to London very early, to see a man about doing a new cookery book called *Great Puds of the Universe*. He absolutely hated baked beans.

Dad was in charge. "I'm on strike," he told the

children. "I can't face another bean in any shape or form." and he got out the frying-pan. "Eggs and bacon, anybody?"

Joss gave her father a pleading look. "But we're nearly there, Dad," she wheedled. "We only need a few more labels. Do fried bread and beans, you love that."

"Not any more, I don't," Mr Shufflebottom said, cracking eggs. "I'm beginning to look like a bean. The top of my head's growing to a point and I'm going this funny orange colour..."

Pin started to cry. "I don't want you to turn into a bean," he yelled. "I want my daddy! I want my mummy! I want my Special Mint Set and I want it now!"

Joss stormed off in disgust. She'd have her coins by now if it wasn't for him cashing in. She pedalled off down to the shop.

Mr Banerjee stuffed six tins of beans into Joss's bag,
purring like a giant cat. "Sure you don't want another
six?" he said. "Offer ends next Tuesday," and he
pointed to the label.

Joss read it, then slunk off. She'd never get the
mint sets now. She felt like crying.

Then a voice said, "Hey, Joss. Come 'ere a minute.
Me 'n' Madge are starvin'. Wot you got in that bag
then?" It was Alfred, the old man who always sat
on the wall opposite Banerjee's. He looked like
someone out of the Bible, with his enormous grey
beard and his long black coat. Madge was little and
round, like a plump pink cushion.

Joss crossed the street and Madge delved nosily
into the shopping bag.

"It's only baked beans," said Joss.

"Hear that, Alf? Only baked beans. This gel doesn't know when she's well off. Baked beans is our favourite. Hey, gel, do you think we could..."

But Joss didn't stay to listen to the rest. Five minutes later she was in the kitchen at home, poring over Mum's *Bean Feast* recipes. She had an idea! She would feed Alfred and Madge on beans!

Alfred loved Mrs Shufflebottom's bean soup; he slurped it down greedily. And Madge was very partial to bean curry. But Joss's biggest success was the bean sandwiches. They actually asked for more.

By lunchtime on Monday Joss had got her hundred labels and she posted them off to Bigga's Beans by Special Express.

Next day she got a phone call. The labels had reached Bigga's Beans in safety and they could expect a surprise visit. Mr Bigga himself was to bring them the two mint sets. "Also," said the voice on the telephone…

Something Else! That night Joss couldn't sleep. Neither could Pin. Mr Bigga, the Beans Person, was all over the television. He didn't just sell beans, he did parachuting and deep-sea diving. He owned an island with palm trees.

"Perhaps he'll take me hunting sharks," Pin said, "or up in his helicopter. D'you think he will?"

No answer. Joss was trying to doze off. She wanted morning to come as quickly as possible.

At eight o'clock next day there was a loud knock on the door. Dad opened it to find a TV camera already filming. Next to it stood Mr Bigga. He was gigantic. So was the cigar he was puffing.

Pin and Joss were pushed forward. "Ah, the two lucky children," he boomed. "Allow me to present your Special Mint Sets. And your special coin books. Applause, please."

Mr Banerjee clapped politely, so did Madge and Alfred. Then Madge pulled at his sleeve. "'Ere, you've not got any of them beans going begging, 'ave you? Only I'm feeling a bit peckish."

"Dear lady," Mr Bigga said grandly, "stand aside if you please. It's time for the *Something Else.*"

Pin and Joss couldn't speak for excitement. Pin was still hoping for a helicopter ride.

But four men in red and yellow uniforms were busy humping cardboard boxes into the front hall.

"What is it?" said Pin.

"Dear boy," said Mr Bigga, "as an extra special thank you to you all for the wisdom you have shown in buying my excellent product, I am giving you, at no extra cost,

A YEAR'S SUPPLY OF ...

BIGGA'S BEST BEANS!"

Acknowledgements

Mary Poggs and the Sunshine
Text © 1993 Vivian French Illustrations © 1993 Colin West

Little Luis and the Bad Bandit
Text © 1993 Ann Jungman Illustrations © 1993 Russell Ayto

"Kari" from *Smart Girls*
Text © 1993 Robert Leeson Illustrations © 1993, 1995 Axel Scheffler

"The Great Golden Belly-button" from *Clever Cakes and Other Stories*
Text © 1991 Michael Rosen Illustrations © 1991 Caroline Holden

Pappy Mashy
Text © 1992 Kathy Henderson Illustrations © 1992 Chris Fisher

Impossible Parents
Text © 1994 Brian Patten Illustrations © 1994 Arthur Robins

A Night to Remember
Text © 1993 Dyan Sheldon Illustrations © 1993 Robert Crowther

Millie Morgan, Pirate
Text © 1992 Margaret Ryan Illustrations © 1992 Caroline Church

The Baked Bean Kids
Text © 1993 Ann Pilling Illustrations © 1993 Derek Matthews